ISHBEL'S CAT

ALAIN GRANT

Illustrated by Annabel Large

SCRIPTURE UNION
130 City Road, London EC1V 2NJ

By the same author: *Wild Cats Never Tame*

First published 1985
Reprinted 1986

ISBN 0 86201 293 7

Phototypeset by Wyvern Typesetting Limited, Bristol
Printed and bound in Great Britain
by Cox & Wyman Ltd, Reading

Contents

To Robin
in gratitude for your careful checking

1 Storm in the forest

Ishbel curled in a ball, drawing the quilt close round her neck. An October gale howled and moaned through the forest, making the straight, dark green pines bow and creak before its mighty power. Four trees had crashed to the ground during the night.

'Birds, you'll be needing breakfast,' Ishbel said, pulling on her clothes.

An icy draught swirled under the back door. Ishbel spooned dripping from the larder bowl into a foil pie dish, crumbled bread on top and took her red anorak from the hook on the kitchen door.

As she turned the knob the door blew inwards, sending her staggering across the floor. She managed to pick up the pie dish from the draining board and fight her way outside, holding the dish close against her so that the bird food didn't blow out.

'Stop it, wind! I've got to shut the door,' she shouted.

The wind whistled rudely, then stopped for a few seconds to let her bang the door shut.

'Thank you,' she yelled, as another gust made

her anorak into a red balloon and tore at her trouser legs.

With head down and body bent, Ishbel pushed her way across the grass to the bird table her father had made. She lifted a heavy stone that kept yesterday's bird dish from blowing away. The dish took off, flying, then bowling across the grass. But Ishbel put her new one on the table and weighted it down with the stone.

Before going back to the house she stood a moment staring at the empty forester's cottage (which was exactly like her own house) on the far side of a rough grass bank.

'Please send a family with children about my age,' she whispered. 'I do hate being the only child this side of the forest.'

There was another gust and what looked like a large dead leaf was carried past Ishbel's face to the ground beside her. She nearly trod on it, but something made her bend and pick it up. It was a wet bundle of feathers – a hen chaffinch which seemed quite dead. Ishbel carried it into the house.

'It's cold and wet – but its little heart is still beating,' said her mother. 'Spread your duffle coat over the chair near the stove and put the bird on it. Then soak some crumbs in a saucer of warm milk. If the little thing gets better it will be starving hungry.'

Ishbel put milk and crumbled bread in a

saucer and Mrs Grant added a trickle of hot
water.

'I'll dish up your porridge,' she said, putting
the bird's saucer on the hob. 'You must be
nearly frozen too.'

While Ishbel was eating there was a thump-
ing on the front door.

'I'll answer it,' she said, running to open up.

A tall man in a black duffle coat stood outside. 'Does James Grant live here?' he asked.

'Yes. But he's out in the forest. Would
Mother do?'

The man nodded. 'I'd like a word with her
before we move our stuff in next door.'

Before fetching her mother Ishbel had a look

at a green van at the gate. There was a woman in it, but no children to be seen.

Mrs Grant and the man talked inside the front door while Ishbel finished breakfast. Then the man went away and Mrs Grant came back.

'Move Dad's chair away, Ishbel,' she said. 'Mr Macdonald's going to bring his boy in for a cup of tea while they get their house warm.'

'How old's the boy?' Ishbel asked.

'A year older than you. But he can't walk. There's something wrong with his legs. He stays in a wheelchair.'

Ishbel felt scared of this strange boy who couldn't walk. She wondered if there were any ordinary children as well.

The front door opened again and the boy was pushed in. Ishbel stared. He was a size smaller than herself. He had a dreamy kind of face, with faraway eyes.

'This is Ishbel, Ian,' Mrs Grant said, helping Ian off with his coat and putting his woolly hat on a peg. 'Would you like some tea to warm you up?'

'Yes, please,' said Ian. 'Hullo, Ishbel.'

'Hullo, Ian,' said Ishbel shyly.

There was a small fuffly noise and Ishbel saw the bird on the chair fluff out its feathers and flutter its wings.

'Why d'you keep a chaffinch in the house?' Ian asked.

Ishbel explained. 'I'll get her food,' she added.

'Look how hungry she is. Her mouth's wide open.'

'That's 'cause she's scared – not hungry,' said Ian, pulling the chaffinch's chair slowly and quietly towards him. 'I'll feed her. Have you a wooden skewer? She'll be too scared to eat from my smelly human fingers.'

He dipped the skewer into the bread Ishbel brought and put a bit into the chaffinch's open beak. Soon the little bird was gobbling down her breakfast. Not long after she was flying round the kitchen and banging herself on the window.

Mrs Grant caught her with a duster and gave

her to Ian to hold. 'It's no good putting her out,' she said. 'I'd better draw the bathroom curtains and clear away the sponges and toothbrushes. It can settle down there by itself.'

'Put a tree branch in the bath so that she'll feel at home there,' Ian suggested.

Ishbel went out, chose a small fallen branch and fitted it into the bath. Ian showed her how to hold the bird gently but firmly with its wings folded and she took it up to the bathroom, shut the door and watched for a few moments through the keyhole.

The chaffinch flew around, then found the branch and settled on it.

Ishbel cleared away the breakfast things so that she and Ian could play Snakes and Ladders while Mrs Grant went next door to help Ian's parents move in.

It was a bit frightening to be left alone in the house with a person who was odd like Ian. Ishbel stole a quick glance at him every time he moved his counter. Only his legs seemed odd. She wanted to ask what was wrong with them – but didn't like to.

'Will you be going to school on Monday?' she asked.

'Yes,' said Ian. 'What's the teacher like?'

'Like my mother,' said Ishbel, laughing. 'She is the teacher, see. There's eleven of us foresters' children in the Primary School. The ones at the High School go by bus. How will you

–' she stopped abruptly and rattled the dice to hide what she'd meant to ask.

'How will I get to school?' Ian finished grumpily. 'Mother'll take me in the van of course.'

Ishbel felt snubbed and they played silently till Ian said: 'Look – we'd better get this straight right away. I was born with a bad back. Lots of people are. So I can't move my legs. Lots of people can't. But I'm *not* batty. Got it? Now let's get on with the game.'

Ishbel didn't know what to say. But she was glad to know. She wasn't scared of Ian any more. In fact she rather liked him.

'You do know how to look after sick birds,' she said admiringly.

Ian smiled and Ishbel felt they were friends.

2 Ian in danger

The wild wind had blown itself out when Ishbel,
Ian, Mrs Grant and Mrs Macdonald went off in
the van along the forest track to school on
Monday. The mothers sat in front and Ishbel sat
on a rug beside Ian.

'Have you still got that chaffinch?' Ian asked.

'No,' said Ishbel. 'It didn't snow like Mother
expected, so we've just let her out. I did want to
keep her – till I had to clear up her messes in the
bathroom. That took ages.'

'She'd have hated living indoors,' said Ian.

After the class had sung the hymn 'All things
bright and beautiful', Mrs Grant asked Ishbel to
tell the others about the chaffinch.

'Can anyone remember what Jesus said about
sparrows?' Mrs Grant asked when Ishbel had
finished.

No hands went up, so she opened the Bible
and read out:

'Jesus said, "Are not two sparrows sold for a
farthing?" – that's a quarter of a penny – "And
one of them shall not fall to the ground without
your Father." What does that mean?'

Ian's hand shot up. 'It means there's a piece

of God in every sparrow.'

'That's one way of putting it, Ian. God has put life into every living thing, hasn't he? So God really cares what happens to birds. He cared so much about the bird that's been living with us that when Ishbel thought it was just a dead leaf, God made her bend down and make sure. But after Jesus had spoken about sparrows, he went on to say that we humans are more important to God than many sparrows. He said God knows everything about each one of us – even the number of hairs on our heads. So you needn't be scared of any predicament you may find your-self in – because God knows what's happening to you every minute of the day. And you're very precious to him. So he's always ready to help you if you ask.'

Ian settled down quickly in school. The other children liked him. They'd have liked him even more if he hadn't been quite so clever and inclined to show off.

Mrs Grant learnt to drive the van, so Mrs Macdonald was able to stay at home and make dinner for Ishbel's father as well as Ian's.

One Thursday afternoon, as they drove home from school, Mrs Grant said: 'The Saturday after next we're going to Inverness to do Christ-mas shopping. Shall we go to the theatre in the afternoon to see Peter Pan?'

There was a chorus of: 'You bet!' and 'Whoopee!' from the back.

'Have you read the book about Peter Pan, Ian?' Mrs Grant asked.

'Mother read it to me years ago. There was a pirate who swallowed a clock, wasn't there?'

'No, sausage!' said Ishbel. 'The *crocodile* swallowed the clock and the *pirate* was terrified of the crocodile because it had bitten off his hand and liked the taste so much it kept chasing him all over the sea so it could eat some more of him.'

When Ishbel woke up on the Tuesday Mrs Grant told her they'd be walking to school because Ian had a cold and wouldn't be going. 'He tends to get quite ill with colds and things,' Mrs Grant explained. 'So he has to stay indoors till he's well again.'

'He'd better be all right by Saturday,' Ishbel said.

But the cold turned out to be measles and by Friday night Ian was very ill with pneumonia.

'I'm afraid no one can go to Inverness,' Mrs Grant said. 'I must help nurse Ian, because his mother can't cope any longer on her own and Dad must finish that fencing on Grandad's farm before the bad weather sets in.'

Ishbel was so angry she nearly cried. '*Stupid* old Ian to have measles *this* week and spoil everything!' she raged. 'Why couldn't he have had it ages ago like me?'

On Saturday morning Ishbel was left alone.

14

So she spent the time sliding down the end of the bath into the water – which wasn't allowed because the bathroom always became a puddle – and sliding down the stairs on an old tray – which wasn't allowed either, because there was no one in the house to pick up the pieces if she hurt herself. Neither game was much fun alone.

Mrs Grant came back for dinner.

'How's Ian?' Ishbel asked sulkily.

Mrs Grant looked round from the stove, her face white and scared.

'I've just cycled over to the McTavish's house to phone the doctor. Ian isn't well at all.'

A horrible empty feeling attacked Ishbel's stomach. She saw the doctor's red car speed past the sitting room window. Then an ambulance came along, stopped a few minutes outside Ian's house and went off again, 'hoo-ha-ing' loudly.

'You said God always looked after people,' Ishbel said angrily. 'But he's forgotten to look after Ian.' Mrs Grant got up from the table.

'*We've* forgotten to ask God to make Ian well,' she said. 'Let's do that now.'

They prayed that Ian would get better, but neither of them wanted any more dinner.

3 Christmas – and a mouse

Mrs Grant gave her head a little shake and got up.

'Come on, Ishbel,' she said. 'Let's cut out a cardboard stage and make cardboard puppets of Peter and Wendy and the others. Ian can have his Peter Pan show after all – when he's better. Just leave the washing up till later.'

'But Ian might not *get* be –.' A lump in her throat stopped Ishbel finishing.

'I'm sure he'll get better,' said Mrs Grant. 'Two things are important when you ask God to do something for you. First you must make sure the thing you ask isn't wrong or selfish. Second, you must trust that God *will* answer your prayer. When you have prayed you must leave the problem to God and do something that takes your mind right off it. I find if I go on thinking about my trouble, then fear comes creeping in. Fear and faith just don't go together, you see.'

They made the stage, Peter, Wendy, a red Indian and Captain Hook, the pirate chief.

After dark, Mrs Macdonald came in.

'Ian's in a little glass cubicle by himself,' she said. 'They've given him a plastic tent with special air inside it and he's better already. Sister says he should be better still tomorrow.'

A week later Ian came home and Ishbel was allowed to spend the whole of Sunday with him. He was nearly well, but very crotchety. He kept her running all over the house and garden for things he wanted. She was quite glad to go back to school next day for a rest.

Instead of seeing the proper play, Peter Pan, in Inverness, Ishbel and Ian cut out more puppets and scenery and gave a show to their parents. It was rather disappointing, but Christmas soon came along to cheer them up.

'Happy Christmas, darling! Time to get going!'

That Christmas morning Ishbel knew there was no stocking at the end of her bed, because all the presents were at the bottom of Grandad's Christmas tree, many miles away.

She fed the birds and sat down to breakfast.

'What time are we starting?' she asked.

'Soon after ten. We'll meet Grannie and Grandad at the church at eleven-thirty.'

'Can I help Ian get ready?'

Mrs Grant brought over a boiled egg and took away the empty porridge plate. 'Yes,' she said. 'But get yourself ready first, won't you?'

'Happy Christmas, Ishbel,' said her father, coming through the kitchen door. He looked unusually tidy in a kilt and tweed jacket. His bushy black beard was neatly trimmed.

Mr Grant was a forester like Ian's father. They worked on a large estate in the Scottish Highlands, planting, cutting down and looking after thousands of pine and larch trees.

Ishbel changed into red corduroy trousers, a new thick white jersey her mother had knitted and shiny black walking shoes. She ran to Ian's house and opened the back door. 'Happy Christmas, everyone!'

A chorus of 'Happy Christmas!' came from the Macdonald family, eating porridge by the kitchen stove.

'Woof!' said a big, grey, hairy dog as he bounced out of a corner, put his front paws on Ishbel's shoulders and licked her cold red nose.

'That's Larry,' said Ian. 'He's Mother's Christmas present to me.'

'Happy Christmas, Larry,' said Ishbel, hugging the jumping, clumsy pup, who was half Old English Sheepdog, half collie and looked like a dirty lamb gone wrong. 'You *are* lucky, Ian. I've never had a pet of my own.'

Soon Ian, Ishbel and her parents went off in the van over a narrow, bumpy road. An hour and twenty minutes later the van growled up a hill to the little church perched on top.

The organ was playing carols when the Grant family opened the door. There were whispers of, 'Happy Christmas, Jamie' as they made their way to the pew.

They'd barely settled themselves, with Ishbel next to her grandad and Ian's chair beside her in the aisle, when the service began with a rousing 'Hark the herald angels sing . . .'

Ishbel shut her eyes and pictured the Christmas tree she'd helped her father load into the van the Saturday before, to go over to Grandad's house. The tree would be standing in Grannie's sitting room – and *what* would be inside those parcels?

A scrabbling sound made her open her eyes in time to see Ian make a grab at the pink tail of his white mouse.

Ian missed and Minky jumped for the neck of a lady in front.

But Minky never reached his landing place. Instead he disappeared into Grandad's large right hand. And Grandad's right hand stayed in his pocket for the rest of the service.

'There must have been little mice in Jesus' stable,' thought Ishbel, 'making nests in the warm straw – perhaps even in the manger where Jesus lay.'

As they sang 'Away in a Manger', the wind was sighing in the pine trees and the church window grew dark.

After church all the Grants and Ian drove to Grandfather's farmhouse. Heavy grey-white clouds covered the sky.

'D'you think it's going to snow?' Ishbel asked.

'I'm sure it is,' said Mrs Grant. 'I wonder if Grandad's got his sheep down or if Dad will have to go after them before he has dinner.'

Grandad's sheep were not all down.

'You just have dinner in peace, Dad,' said Ishbel's father. 'I'll take Donald and have the rest of the flock in the bottom pasture in no time.'

He stepped into his father's boots, took a thick coat off the peg, the crook from its corner and whistled up Donald the sheepdog from the yard.

'I'll come with you,' Ishbel shouted, pulling on her grannie's coat and boots and running after him.

First they counted the sheep in the lower

field. Fifteen were missing – mostly ignorant lambs who had not yet known a winter. Then Ishbel and her father trudged up the steep grassy hill till they reached a path through the heather.

The keen wind blew in their faces. Donald's eyes were almost shut, his ears were back and his tail drooped as he kept to Mr Grant's heels.

'Keep close behind me, Ishbel,' Mr Grant shouted, 'so I make a wind shield for you.'

Ishbel laughed. 'Mark my footsteps, good my page . . .' she sang merrily, stamping time to the King Wenceslas carol. She ran into her father's back and put a clumsy foot on Donald's paw as Mr Grant stopped abruptly.

'Wait here,' he shouted, 'Old Babsie's sheltering behind those stones. I'll just check she's OK.'

He was soon back. 'She's all right. You can collect her on the way down.'

Nine sheep were huddled together on the far side of the first hill. Mr Grant sent Donald to get them.

'Look – there's the others,' shouted Ishbel. 'I'll get that lot.'

As she clumped down in Grannie's too-big boots it grew dark and scary. Then the sun shone brilliantly through a crack in the clouds before disappearing again. The sudden glory of the sky took Ishbel by surprise. She lifted her face, expecting to see angels as the shepherds had on that first Christmas Eve, tripped over a dead heather stem and fell flat on her stomach.

'Hold up, clumsy,' laughed her father as he helped her up. 'If we don't hurry there'll be no goose left.'

When they reached the house they found double helpings of everything on two plates in the oven.

'I'm sorry we had to start,' Grannie said. 'The bird would have been horribly over-cooked if we'd waited longer.'

Ishbel hardly heard. She sat facing the Christmas tree, which glittered in the dark, uncurtained window. Above it Grannie had fixed a turnip lantern which lit three doll angels with goose-feather wings, floating on invisible threads. Ishbel imagined she was back on the hill in that sudden gleam of sun.

She understood the story of the shepherds and the angels better than ever before.

'Eat up, dreamer,' said her mother. 'You're not doing justice to Grannie's beautiful goose.'

Ishbel came to earth with a bump. 'Oh, Grannie – it's not my darling Gloriana Goose we're eating, is it?'

Grannie smiled. 'Certainly not. Gloriana's going to lay next year's goslings. You can take her some goodies after you've finished dinner.'

When crackers had been pulled and parents and grandparents were nibbling nuts and chatting, Ishbel winked at Ian and stole quietly out.

A few minutes later she came in backwards, holding out an enticing apple core.

Behind waddled an enormous white goose. She wore a green and red paper bonnet. Green beads hung round her neck and from her mouth hung a ribbon of apple peel. Red and green tinsel adorned her tail, trailing like a bridal train behind her.

'Take her out quick,' Grannie ordered when the laughter had died down. 'I know something terrible's going to happen any minute now!'

4 Elspeth comes but Fiona goes missing

Ian had an enormous parcel under the Christmas tree. He and Ishbel unwrapped it, to find a black and green toboggan with a shaped, padded back and hand-worked brake. Ian couldn't go racing down bumpy hills in case he damaged his back – but this machine would let him share the snow and fun with the other children.

'I knew Dad was doing something special in the shed,' he said, his grin spreading almost from ear to ear. 'I'll make Larry a sledge dog harness.'

Ishbel's biggest parcel had wooden skis in it, which Grandad had made many years ago for her father when he was Ishbel's age. Her second largest contained red wooden ski sticks.

When she'd opened all her presents she realised there had been nothing from her mother, who had disappeared.

The door was flung open. Mrs Grant came in carrying a covered basket. The scarf covering it moved in an odd, jerky way.

'Open it quick!' said Mrs Grant as a tiny fluffy paw poked out.

'It's a *kitten*! Oh I've longed and longed for

you, little one!'

Ishbel hugged the scrap of grey tabby fur.
The kitten stuck tiny pins into her shoulder.
'You're Elspeth,' Ishbel murmured. 'I've
pretended you for years and years. You're even
prettier than I pretended. I do hope it snows
tonight!'

'Don't worry,' grumbled her grandfather. 'It
will.'

Grandad dreaded the snow that year. He'd
had a tractor accident during the summer
which badly damaged one knee. Ishbel's father
had come over every weekend since to help
with jobs that were too difficult and painful for
Grandad to do. Winter was hard for farmers in

26

the Highlands, especially if they were unfit or old.

The party broke up early because snow started falling.

Ishbel went to bed with Elspeth curled up between the two top blankets, while huge snow flakes fell silently outside.

The bedroom door was open. In the dim light from downstairs she gazed at a picture on the opposite wall of Jesus, the Good Shepherd, leading a small flock of sheep and carrying a lamb in his arms.

'Thank you, Jesus,' she whispered, 'for a lovely Christmas, and my presents – especially Elspeth. And for making Ian well so he was at Grandad's too. It is *fun* being a shepherd, isn't it, Jesus?'

Three days after New Year, Ishbel, Mrs Grant and Ian started school again.

There was a tremendous wind. The pine trees bowed and tossed their heads. The van slid and bumped over frozen snow.

The others were already in school when they arrived – everyone but Fiona Stewart.

'Anyone know if Fiona's ill?' Mrs Grant asked.

'She brought my mum's eggs this morning,' said Alan Cameron.

'Why didn't she come with you, then?'

Alan's freckled face went red. He found Fiona boring, so he'd run on directly he saw her coming towards their house.

'I – I'd already started,' he said.

Mrs Grant gave ten-year-old Alan a withering look. 'So you were a perfect gentleman and left a little girl of seven to come alone – when branches were blowing all over the place,' said Mrs Grant sarcastically.

Alan looked uncomfortable.

'Sorry, Mrs Grant,' he mumbled.

'I hope you are,' said Mrs Grant, getting into her coat again. 'Stick on your wellies and cap and coat, Alan. Come and show me the short cut to your house. Billy Douglas, take the register and see everyone has a book to look at and keeps quiet till we're back. Moira – you can help Billy keep order.'

As Alan and Mrs Grant set out through the forest it started snowing hard. Alan kept a lookout on the left of the path while Mrs Grant searched the right side.

But they hadn't found her when they reached Alan's house.

And Fiona wasn't at the house.

'She ran after you, Alan,' said Mrs Cameron. 'Didn't you hear her calling?'

Alan's face went red again. 'How could I hear in that gale?' he asked.

Mrs Cameron grabbed her coat and boots. 'I'll come back with you,' she said.

Alan, his mother and Mrs Grant walked back along the short cut to school. Snow covered the

narrow path. Fiona could easily have missed her way.

'You walk slowly along the path, Alan,' said Mrs Cameron. 'We'll go through the forest on either side.'

They called Fiona's name as they went, stopping to listen for her answer. But the wind's racket drowned their voices.

Mrs Grant saw something red poking between two tree trunks. A fallen branch lay near it on the ground. She rushed over and saw that it was Fiona's woolly hat. Fiona's tear-stained face and big frightened eyes peeped out of her grey duffle coat beneath it. She lay against a white mound of snow. Her coat and black wellies were almost buried.

'Fiona darling!' Mrs Grant gathered the little girl into her arms.

'Oo – my elbow!' Fiona screamed.

'That branch must have hit the child's arm as it fell,' said Mrs Grant as Alan and his mother came up.

Mrs Cameron fetched Fiona's mother while Mrs Grant carried the shivering, sobbing child to the Camerons' house.

Alan piled logs on the kitchen stove and brought dry clothes while Mrs Grant carefully took off Fiona's wet ones. Soon her parents came and took the little girl to the doctor to have her arm seen to.

'If Fiona had died in the snow it would have

been your fault, Alan,' said Mrs Cameron sternly.

Back at school Alan had to listen while Mrs Grant told the other children what had happened.

'We all have to help one another,' she said, 'especially in winter. Everyone in the world belongs to God's great big family. It's the job of each one of us to keep others around us from coming to harm – especially if they're younger than we are.'

School finished early and Mrs Grant walked home with the four children who lived in cottages close by. Then she made the others pile into the van and drove them home before going on with Ishbel and Ian.

Ian spied a fluttering movement in the snow as his chair was pushed towards his front door.

'Look, Ishbel, that's another fallen bird,' he said.

Ishbel scooped it up with her mittened hands.

Inside the house she laid it on Ian's knee and he gently brushed the snow off a half-frozen hedge-sparrow. The bird flapped feebly but was too cold and tired to hop off Ian's knee. Ian opened his coat and nestled the bird between his warm neck and the collar of his jersey.

'Is it too far gone?' Ishbel asked.

'Not too far gone for me to revive,' said Ian, smiling.

That night Ishbel and her mother thanked God for keeping Fiona safe in the snow till she was found.

'And thank you for making Ian see that sparrow,' Ishbel added. 'Mother!' she exclaimed, 'It *was* a sparrow that fell to the ground this time – just like Jesus said.'

'So it was. But Fiona is more important than many sparrows.'

'God must be angry with Alan for not waiting for Fiona,' said Ishbel.

'I'm sure he was. But when poor Alan understood his unkindness led to Fiona's broken arm and gave her an awful fright he was very sorry and ashamed. God forgives us when we are really sorry for what we've done, doesn't he? If he didn't, then you and I would find ourselves in a lot of trouble, wouldn't we?'

Ishbel snuggled under her quilt. 'I don't think Fiona will *ever* forgive Alan,' she said.

5 Grandad is lost in the snow

There was deep snow in the forest for six weeks. Every weekend the children skied on a hill near the school. Ian, looking like an eskimo in a nylon fur suit and cap, came to train Larry as a sledge dog.

Before Larry was harnessed, Ishbel always took him for a romp. He would bound around, pulling his long legs out of the deep holes they made, scuffing snow into her face while she pelted him with snowballs.

It took him a while to get the idea of sledge pulling, so Ian and his sledge fetched up in some comic places – wrapped round a tree or half-way into a ditch. But there were plenty of laughing children to rescue him.

At the farm Grandad limped around carrying heavy loads of food to his sheep, and Grannie wore herself out sharing his work and getting through her own as well.

Then warmer weather came and snow turned into murky water. Ishbel went to sleep listening to the drip, drip from the pine branches.

Grandad's sheep wandered away from the

lower pasture to nibble grass in the squelchy ground higher up.

Then the west wind blew. White snow flakes floated down for four days and nights.

The foresters couldn't work. Ishbel, Ian and Mrs Grant couldn't get to school. Snow crawled up the sides of Ishbel's house and her father had a battle each morning to get the back door open and a path dug to his log store.

Mr Grant wondered if his father's sheep were buried under snow-drifts – but the roads were blocked so he couldn't get to the farm and help.

An hour after dark one day there was banging on the back door and Mr Mackintosh – owner of the forest – walked in.

'I came to tell you, Jamie,' he said, 'that they were out looking for your father till the light failed. He went off just after dinner to feed the sheep. Two hours later the dog came back without him.'

Ishbel's father went straight up to Mr Mackintosh's house so that he could keep in touch with his mother and the search party's police station by telephone.

By first light next morning the snow had stopped and the men went out again to search for Grandad. They found that he had gone to sleep in the snow and wouldn't be waking up again.

'Will Grandad be in heaven already? Will I never see him again – ever?' Ishbel whispered tearfully when her mother said goodnight.

'One day you will, darling. One day all our family will be together in heaven. Jesus himself promised this to everyone who believes in God and in Jesus.'

Ishbel rubbed behind Elspeth's ear, thinking of the long years she'd have to wait before she was old and could meet Grandad again.

Next day snow ploughs cleared the road and Mr Mackintosh drove Mr Grant to his father's farm. Ishbel's father was away ten days, digging out starving half-buried sheep and working on the farm that now belonged to him. It was to be the Grants' new home.

Ishbel just didn't know *how* she was going to say goodbye to her forest home, her human, animal and bird friends and, worst of all, Ian.

'Soon you'll be the only friend I have, Elspeth,' she said.

A teacher was found to run the school and, one frosty morning, Ishbel said goodbye to Ian and watched him go off to school with his mother.

She gazed tearfully at the forest she'd known and loved all her life.

'Goodbye, Ishbel,' the forest was saying. 'You don't belong here any more.'

Wheels scrunched on frosty snow. Ishbel looked round to see her father jump out of Grandad's Land Rover.

She ran and hugged him. 'Dad, you've been

away *ages*. Are we going now – this minute?'

'As soon as we get the suitcases and urgent things loaded in. I'll borrow a truck and fetch the rest later.'

Ishbel was wedged between suitcases and nearly smothered under quilts, coats and blankets.

At the farm not only Grandad was missing, but Grannie too.

'She's having a rest with Aunt Shona in Edinburgh,' Mr Grant explained. 'So you'll be run off your feet helping me outside and Mother in the kitchen. Donald! Where are you, you lazy hound?'

'Don't call him, Jamie. Come and look.' Mrs Grant was shaking with silent laughter.

The old dog, who could terrify a flock of sheep with his fierce eyes, was cowering inside the back door. In the doorway, between Donald and his new master, stood one angry kitten.

Elspeth, with every bit of fur fluffed out, looked twice her normal size. Her tail was like a grey bottle brush, her ears laid back. Her little mouth, with its wicked kitten teeth, was wide open, hissing hatred.

Ishbel grabbed the furious cat, who struggled, scratching, out of her arms and scampered into the living room. 'Poor old Donald! And I'd been scared you might eat Elspeth!'

Donald gave Ishbel a grateful lick on the hand as he ran out to join his new master.

Ishbel was run off her feet that first week. There were so many mouths to feed.

Mr Grant fed the sheep and cattle. Mrs Grant fed the human family. Ishbel fed everyone else.

Elspeth needed breakfast, dinner and tea. Donald had dinner. Gloriana Goose and Gordon Gander, Corker the cock and his twenty-one wives, Derek the drake and eleven ducks had breakfast and tea thrown to them outside.

A week after they'd moved, Mrs Grant drove Ishbel to her new school.

The school seemed huge, smelt unfriendly and nearly deafened her with its noise. She shared a desk with a cross-looking girl called Natalie.

The teacher's name was Miss Thursday. Ishbel named her 'Blue Thursday' (because she had blue thick-rimmed spectacles) and didn't think they'd like each other.

Natalie kept whispering, which made Blue Thursday turn and fix Ishbel with a black stare from her blue spectacles.

The fourth time Natalie whispered Ishbel got angry and whispered: 'Shut up!'

Of course Blue Thursday caught her at it. 'I'll have *no* whispering in my class, Ishbel Grant,' she thundered. 'Do it once more and there'll be trouble!'

Next time Miss Thursday turned her back Natalie spiked Ishbel in the bottom with something sharp. Ishbel jumped – but gritted her teeth and kept silent. The rest of the class giggled.

'I *hate* that school,' Ishbel complained when she got home. 'I hate the girl at my desk most of all.'

'Strangers are always horrible,' said Mrs Grant. 'Get to know them and you'll find they're nearly all nice.'

'How do I get to know *them* when they don't want to know *me*?' Ishbel asked despairingly a week later. 'Ian must be very lonely without me next door.'

'Oh, I never told you,' said Mrs Grant, 'there's a new family now in our old house. Two boys a year or two older than Ian – and a baby girl. Isn't that lucky?'

'Everyone's lucky but me,' Ishbel told Elspeth sourly in bed that night.

6   Unfair punishment

In March, when the mornings were light, Ishbel walked down the farm track to the school bus stop.

She didn't notice one day as she waited for the bus that a small animal was waiting near, behind the clump of heather. When she boarded the bus no one saw the animal jump in and hide under the back seat.

Later, when Blue Thursday strode into class and the English lesson started, Ishbel felt prickles sticking into her right knee. As she squirmed and looked down Elspeth jumped into her lap.

Swallowing her amazement, Ishbel wiggled herself and Elspeth further under the desk. Elspeth lay down purring happily.

Blue Thursday told the children to get out their dictation books. Natalie dropped hers. As she scrabbled for it on the floor Elspeth combed her hair with a paw.

Ishbel snatched away the paw, but tugged a lock of hair too.

Natalie jumped and banged her head on the desk, while Ishbel clung desperately to the frightened kitten.

'Please Miss Thursday, could you wait? I dropped my book,' said Natalie.

'That's your fault,' said Miss Thursday, going on dictating.

'What have you got on your knee?' asked Natalie, trying to see.

Ishbel put Natalie's hand on Elspeth's furry back. 'Sh-sh,' she ordered.

'Natalie! Ishbel! *What* are you two playing at?' Still dictating Blue Thursday marched down the line and peered at Ishbel's desk. The gold-coloured chain round Miss Thursday's neck dangled temptingly. Elspeth's eyes gleamed. She put out a paw and patted it – then sprang on to the teacher's shoulder.

Blue Thursday jumped back – her face a sickly greenish white. 'Take it away,' she breathed faintly, clutching the desk.

'It's only a kitten,' said Ishbel, picking Elspeth off her teacher's shoulder.

'Get it out,' screeched Miss Thursday. 'I can't stand cats!'

Someone opened the door. Ishbel ran out, carrying Elspeth, straight into the head teacher.

'Sorry, Miss Gimbal, I didn't see you,' she whispered.

'Ishbel Grant, *what* are you doing with that kitten?'

'It – it came into our classroom.'

'Give it to me. I'll put it outside.'

'Oh no, please, Miss Gimbal. She's *my* kitten. She'd get lost.'

'Surely you know you aren't allowed to bring animals to school?' inquired Miss Gimbal.

'I didn't bring her. She brought herself. She must have followed me.'

Miss Gimbal looked doubtfully at Ishbel. 'Then she will stay in my room till you go home this afternoon. And see she *never* follows you again!'

Blue Thursday was most unpleasant the rest of the day.

That night Ishbel told Jesus about her troubles at school. 'I don't think I'll *ever* get on with Blue Thursday, however hard I try. And I haven't a single friend. Please find me just one friend, Jesus. Then I won't mind everything else!'

Next morning started with number work. Natalie was useless at number work and very slow. She was a page behind Ishbel in the book, so every time Ishbel needed to copy a sum she had to turn the page over. Natalie got fed up with turning it back again so she held the page down with her right hand while she wrote with her left – and wouldn't let Ishbel turn over.

Ishbel clutched the book and tried to ease Natalie's hand off it.

Natalie flew into a rage and snatched with both hands – but Ishbel didn't let go.

43

The book, well-used and tatty, came apart with a splitting sound. Both girls overbalanced on the floor, each clinging to half the book.

The class burst out laughing.

'Ishbel! Natalie! Come up here, both of you.' Blue Thursday's face was crimson with anger. 'You've destroyed an *expensive* book.' She held up the two halves for the class to see. 'You will stay here *every* break until you've each copied one half of it. Then you can help me stick the halves together. And you, Ishbel, will take home this book you've spoilt. Your mother can repair it.'

Ishbel and Natalie spent nine break times copying that dreadful book. Ishbel hated being alone with Natalie, copying boring figures.

'Why did you have to come to my school and get me into all this trouble,' Natalie asked angrily the first day.

'Because Grandad died in the snow – so Dad had to come and look after his farm. I didn't *want* to come to this school. My old school was *nice.*'

'Was your grandad Mr Grant of Corrieneuk?'

'That's right.'

'Neuk means death, doesn't it?' said Natalie spitefully. 'Your dad'll probably die in the snow one day. My grannie says that's why your glen is called 'neuk'. People have died there before.'

'Then you can just tell your grannie it was called Corrieneuk 'cause two men had a fight

there hundreds of years ago and one got killed –
so there! Where do you live?'

'Half a mile this side of Corrieneuk. Grannie
keeps chickens and breeds King Charles
spaniels.'

'What does your dad do?' Ishbel asked.

'He hasn't a job. Mum has though – office
cleaning. They live in Manchester.'

'Why don't you live with them?'

' 'Cause Mum didn't look after me proper. So
Grannie fetched me here.'

'Don't your mum and dad want you back?'

Natalie shrugged. 'They're not bothered.'

Ishbel told her parents about Natalie at
tea-time.

'That explains why Natalie's nasty,' said Mrs
Grant. 'Nasty people are often the way they are
because someone's been nasty to them. Do you
know the only sure way to defeat your enemies,
Ishbel?'

'No. How do I?'

'Make them into friends.'

Ishbel laughed scornfully. She couldn't see
herself wanting Natalie for a friend.

'I remember Natalie's mother when I was at
school,' said Mr Grant. 'A stupid little girl she
was. Her mother was nice though – the grannie
Natalie lives with.'

Next day Ishbel slipped four toffees into her
jersey pocket.

'My dad remembers your mum at school,

Natalie,' she said as they started copying out the book.

Natalie didn't answer.

'Dad remembers your grannie, too.'

Still no answer.

'Would you like a toffee?'

'What d'you think?' said Natalie.

Ishbel handed her a toffee and sucked one herself.

'D'you like living here better than Manchester?'

'What d'you think?' said Natalie through the toffee.

'I wouldn't know. I've never been to Manchester.'

'It's always raining there. It's dirty – and nothing but buildings. I hate it.'

'Has your grannie any King Charles puppies?'

'Yes. Like to see them sometime?'

'Yes!'

As they went out of school that Friday afternoon Natalie said: 'Want to see the puppies tomorrow?'

'Yes, please,' said Ishbel. 'What time?'

'After breakfast.'

Mr Grant dropped Ishbel at Natalie's house. Natalie showed her two families of puppies.

'Aren't they cuddly?' Ishbel squatted in the middle of the older family, which jumped all over her.

'Yes. We won't have any of that lot left by this time next week. It's awful sad when they go away.'

After dinner they took Natalie's own six month old puppy for a training walk.

Natalie was different at home with the dogs and her grannie.

Next day the Grants went to the church they'd last been to on Christmas day. Christmas seemed a very long time ago. Ishbel had to be nudged every time she was supposed to stand or sit down because her mind was thinking of the great hill of happenings between Christmas and that present March Sunday.

Ishbel's family had been moved all over the place – like counters in a game of Snakes and Ladders.

Grandad had gone shooting up a ladder to heaven. Grannie had slid down a snake to Edinburgh. Ishbel and her parents had been moved from their forest. Ian hadn't moved at all.

'You were a long way off in church this morning,' Mr Grant teased as they had dinner.

'I was thinking of the sort of Snakes and Ladders game God was playing with our family,' Ishbel said.

'God doesn't play games with us – all depending on luck,' said Mrs Grant. 'He's got things planned out for us. As long as we obey him, every move is a good one for us in the end – though we may not approve of it at the time. He can bring good out of anything. Did you remember to thank him for bringing you a friend when you were lonely?'

'No,' said Ishbel. 'I forgot. He took an awful long time doing that, didn't he? And getting me a punishment for something that wasn't my fault was a funny way to do it.'

Mrs Grant laughed. 'God's ways often seem strange to us. But he sees the future and we only see the right now. That's what makes the difference.'

When the number work book was at last copied out and the girls took it to Blue

Thursday, Ishbel said with a wicked grin: 'Thank you, Miss Thursday, for giving us such a useful punishment.'

Miss Thursday was most surprised. 'Are you being cheeky, Ishbel?'

'Oh no,' said Ishbel. 'You see me and Natalie hated each other till we copied that nasty book. Now we're friends.'

A glimmer of a smile came to Miss Thursday's face. 'Does that mean you'll be whispering to each other *all* the time instead of just some of the time?' she asked.

Elspeth never went to school again – but she had other adventures and got Ishbel into all kinds of trouble rescuing her.

One Saturday when there was a thin layer of ice over a wide, lazy stretch of the river that bubbled busily between rocks below the farm, Elspeth scampered over it. The ice gave way. A scared-to-death Elspeth splashed and scrabbled in the water.

Of course Ishbel followed. She got soaked, frozen and narrowly escaped being drowned.

Another day Elspeth caught one back foot in a rabbit snare. Ishbel was nearly scratched to pieces before she managed to free her kitten.

One early summer night Elspeth went missing altogether. Long after Ishbel's parents and grannie (who was living at the farm again) were asleep in bed, Ishbel heard a mournful 'Mee-ow' and went out to find Elspeth stuck up a high tree.

Ishbel climbed after her and got stuck herself for the rest of the night. No one heard *her* shouts for help till her father came out to milk the cows.

'That cat will kill you one day,' said Mr Grant furiously. 'We'd better find another home for her.'

'You needn't worry about *me*,' said Ishbel. 'Whenever I'm in a fix I ask Jesus to keep me safe. He always does.'

'It's time you learnt to ask Jesus what to do *before* you get in a fix,' said her mother. 'Try asking him and then waiting quietly for a few minutes. If you'd done that last night he might have put it into your mind to ask Dad to rescue Elspeth.'

'Why does Jesus *make* Elspeth get me into trouble?' Ishbel asked thoughtfully. 'Why did he make Ian be born with legs that don't work? Why does he make so many sad, bad things happen?'

'D'you remember the story Jesus told about the man who sowed good seed in his field? In the night an enemy crept in and sowed weeds among the wheat. Jesus said he himself was the sower of the good seed. D'you remember who the enemy was?'

'That was the devil,' said Ishbel.

Mrs Grant nodded. 'The enemy still keeps

spoiling Jesus' work and hurting people Jesus loves. If only people read and understood the Bible better, they wouldn't be always blaming God for the evil things that happen to them.'

7   Lost in the Glen of Death

Every fine morning of the summer holidays Ishbel and Natalie took hard-boiled eggs, cheese sandwiches and oranges out with them.

They wandered in the heather around the farm or sat talking in the sun while Natalie's puppy, Kerry, went looking for rabbits and Elspeth hunted mice.

'Let's go on a long hike tomorrow,' Natalie suggested one day, 'in the hills over there.' She pointed across the river. 'Let's be explorers – like David Livingstone.'

'Can I have an extra egg and some Kendalmint, Mother?' Ishbel asked next morning. 'Nallie and me are going exploring.'

'Where are you exploring?' Mrs Grant asked quickly.

'Africa,' said Ishbel, pointing. 'Over there across the Amazon.'

Mrs Grant laughed. 'It's the Nile you'll be crossing, not the Amazon. See you're home by six. And take your anorak!'

'It's boiling *hot*!'

'The weather changes quicker here than where we used to live.'

' 'Bye then. See you tea-time – if we're not eaten by lions.' Ishbel and Elspeth started off down the track to meet Natalie.

'Shall we go over the road bridge or the narrow bridge down the glen?' she asked Natalie when they met.

'The glen bridge is shorter – and nicer.'

Mrs Grant waved as they passed the house. She saw them cross the bridge and turn south along the river bank.

'Just *look* at that!' Ishbel exploded, pointing.

Natalie looked up from watching trout scudding around in the water.

'That's a *new* fence,' she exploded. 'Pigs! What did they want to put that up for?'

'To keep us out,' said Ishbel sulkily. 'They had hundreds of trees burnt last year – people were careless with cigarette ends. I bet that fence goes right down the glen.'

It did. There was no way to the African mountains.

'Let's explore Russia on the other side of the river then,' said Natalie.

They found a ford of huge stones that stood above the frothing water.

'They look awfully slippery,' said Ishbel.

'Chicken! They're easy if you hold on with your hands.'

'What about Elspeth and Kerry?'

'We'll put them in the haversacks and tie their leads tight round our middles.'

'Where does the food go?'

'What you got a mouth for?'

Five minutes later the explorers started to cross the Nile.

Kerry struggled and yelped in Natalie's haversack, but Elspeth snuggled down happily, licking up crumbs from yesterday's sandwiches.

Natalie sprang neatly across. Ishbel followed. One foot slithered into the water and she nearly dropped the food bag from her teeth – but her hands held firm.

They sat in warm heather to wring out shoes and socks, free the animals and recover their breath.

Then they set off up the first hill on a sheep track. There was a higher hill behind it. And yet a third behind that.

'Let's have a bite before we start up that one,' said Ishbel.

They'd eaten their dinner on top of the first hill.

'We're not climbing that one,' said Natalie. 'See what the time is?'

Ishbel looked at her watch. 'Nearly half past four. We'll never make it home by six!'

'See those clouds? Better get going – fast! Come on, Kerry.'

'Elspeth! Elspeth!' Ishbel called.

But Elspeth was nowhere.

Ishbel and Natalie hunted for her for half an hour. But she'd clean disappeared.

'We *must* go,' said Natalie. 'It's getting dangerous.'

'But I can't leave Elspeth. She'll never find her way home.'

'She will. She's a cat.'

'She's a kitten! There's foxes at night – and eagles. And –'

'And *us*,' Natalie shouted. '*You* can die in the hills if you like. Come on, Kerry.'

She put Kerry on the lead and ran downhill.

'Elspeth! Elspeth! *Please* come.'

Ishbel waited a few more minutes. Then followed Natalie.

About half-way down – quite suddenly – they

couldn't see their way at all.

'Where's this fog come from?' Ishbel demanded.

'Wind's blowing banks of clouds over. Didn't you notice?'

'I was looking for Elspeth. Could a fox have got her already?'

But Natalie was out of sight. So was the path.

'Hi! Wait for me.' Ishbel stumbled on through bumpy heather. '*Please* God, keep Elspeth safe,' she begged.

The fog was like a nightmare you struggled to wake up from, but didn't. Suddenly she was out of it, near the bottom of the valley. She saw Natalie far away to her left.

Natalie waved and waited.

'I missed the path,' Ishbel panted.

'So did I,' said Natalie. 'D'you know which of those hills is Hill One?'

Ishbel looked at the two hills. They looked alike – at the bottom. The top half of both was covered in cloud.

'They look just the same, Nallie – with their white hats on.'

'Cloud-covered hills always do. You only know hills by the shapes of their tops.'

'I think the right one is Hill One,' said Ishbel.

Natalie agreed.

They started up the hill but were soon lost in mist again.

Ishbel fell over a jutting piece of rock and cut

her leg. 'Hill One wasn't rocky,' she said, rubbing away the tickly blood which ran down.

'I think it was rocky in some places,' Natalie said uncertainly. 'Ow!' She stumbled and fell.

Ishbel fell over her.

'Why are you lying down?' she asked crossly.

'I – put my foot – in a hole,' Natalie sobbed. 'My ankle – twisted.'

She stood up a few minutes later. But walking was almost impossible. The ankle was too sore.

'The mist's getting darker,' she said. 'We'd better stay here.'

'Stay *here*? Till when?'

'Till we can see. Grannie made me promise never to go on walking when I can't see. It's too dangerous. You can walk over the edge.'

'But it'll be dark soon. We can't stay here all night.'

'Why not?'

'It's cold and – scary.'

'So what? I'd rather be cold and alive – wouldn't you?'

'Let's eat something,' said Ishbel.

'I haven't any food left.'

'I've another egg and some Kendalmint.' Ishbel peeled the egg and halved it. 'I s'pose we'd better keep the Kendalmint till later.'

'We might crawl round this rock and get out of the wind,' Natalie said when they'd finished eating.

There was a ghostly screech above their

heads. Ishbel nearly jumped off the hill. 'What's that?' she whispered.

'Only an owl. Let's lie down in the heather – tight together so it's warmer.'

'We could shout. *Someone* might hear!'

'Some hope!' said Natalie bitterly. 'No one ever comes when *I* shout.'

They shouted themselves hoarse. No one came.

'Were you out on the hills all night before, then?' Ishbel asked.

'No. But my mum and dad sometimes locked me in our flat and went to parties,' said Natalie. 'I got scared and yelled. But no one ever came.'

Ishbel shut her eyes. 'Please, *please* God,' she begged, 'get us home soon. And please make Elspeth come home too.'

'That won't get you anywhere,' said Natalie. 'Oh help! I forgot.'

'Forgot what?'

'We're in Corrieneuk – the Glen of Death. We *are* going to die!' Natalie started a small, strange, eerie wailing which went on – and on – and on . . .

But Ishbel was already asleep.

The sun rose red in the mist. The girls were still asleep. A rabbit popped his head out of a hole, nibbled some wisps of grass and popped back again. Then a furry, sand-coloured animal limped over the heather and lay down by Ishbel's neck.

A cock grouse landed to feed. Kerry's nose caught the smell of him.

'Ow! Ow! Ow!' said Kerry, bouncing up to give chase.

Natalie started up. 'Wake up quick. It's getting light. Look Ishbel! Elspeth's back!'

Ishbel opened her eyes. 'Elspeth *darling*. She's all orangey-yellow! Where on *earth* have you been, Elspeth?'

'She'll have got lost down a rabbit hole – that's what. One of Grannie's pups did – and he was just the same colour.'

'What's that huge red ball, Nallie?'

'The sun of course. It's red 'cause we're inside mist and the sun's outside it. Look – the mist's thinner. We'll see the way soon.'

But when the cloud lifted they still didn't know where they were.

Suddenly Elspeth started trotting downhill in a very determined way.

'That's Elspeth's going home trot,' said Ishbel. 'She'll show us the way.'

Elspeth led and the others followed – Natalie rather slowly because her ankle had only half recovered.

About an hour later they were shouting and waving at someone who stood in front of Ishbel's house.

She turned round. Kerry, Elspeth and Ishbel galloped towards her. Natalie limped behind.

'Grannie!'

As Ishbel ran into her arms Grannie burst into tears.

'Wherever have you been?' she asked. 'Jamie and Anne – and the Mountain Rescue – have searched the hills all night. We must phone the police so that everyone can go home.'

'Can I phone Grannie?' asked Natalie.

'Your grannie's asleep upstairs. She was searching too.'

They had hot baths and a hot breakfast. Ishbel began to dread her parents coming back.

She heard the Land Rover and rushed out to greet them, not wanting to be scolded in front of Natalie.

'I'm sorry. I'm awfully, awfully sorry.' Fearfully she told them how it had been Elspeth's fault this time too.

Mrs Grant's face went pink and her blue eyes seemed to snap.

But Mr Grant butted in quietly: 'No, Anne, don't blame the child. It was natural she should hunt for Elspeth, and Ishbel isn't yet used to this kind of country.' He turned to Ishbel. 'You and I will do a bit of training now you live in the hills. But where on earth *did* you get to?'

Ishbel explained.

'But you were going into the small hills the *other* side of the river. You saw them cross the bridge, Anne.'

'We couldn't get up those hills, Dad, because of the new fence. So we came back across the ford.

Mr Grant still looked mystified. 'But you can still get straight into those hills from the road – the fence doesn't block the path there.'

'They crossed the river by the *glen* bridge, Jamie,' said Mrs Grant. 'I'd no idea there was a new fence the other side.'

Mr Grant's face changed. 'Good heavens, child – you weren't up in the high hills right down there! Don't you *ever* go into hills like that again without an adult! And from now on you will not go anywhere without telling one of us exactly where you'll be. Understood?'

Ishbel nodded. 'Understood, Dad.'

'You know something, Mother,' Ishbel said that evening when she got into bed. 'I asked God last night to get us home again. And to make Elspeth come home too. Nallie said asking him wouldn't do any good. But he *did* get us and Elspeth home.'

'He did indeed, darling. Remind Nallie about that. Isn't it wonderful to know that he's ready to help whenever we ask?'

'Why doesn't Nallie know that?' said Ishbel.

'Maybe no one's ever told her,' Mrs Grant replied.

If you have enjoyed this story, you might like to read more about Ishbel and Elspeth in 'Wild Cats Never Tame'.

Wild Cats never Tame
Alain Grant

The Scottish wild cat is the wildest and most untameable of animals. Ishbel's cat, Elspeth, mates with a wild cat.

Cluny is the only survivor of the litter and Ishbel sets her heart on taming this wild kitten.

But Cluny is quite determined not to trust any humans. He soon discovers that nature is just as hostile.